My Dearest Dinosaur

by Margaret Wild

illustrated by Donna Rawlins

ORCHARD BOOKS · NEW YORK

The author and illustrator wish to thank the following people for their generous consultation and advice—Robert Jones, Collections Manager, Earth Sciences, The Australian Museum, Sydney; Dr. Mark Hutchinson, Curator of Reptiles and Amphibians, South Australian Museum, Adelaide; and John Scanlon of the University of New South Wales.

Orchard Books, 95 Madison Avenue, New York, NY 10016

Manufactured in the United States of America. Printed by Barton Press, Inc.
Bound by Horowitz/Rae. Book design by Mina Greenstein.
The text of this book is set in 16 point Usherwood Medium. The illustrations are drawn and painted with colored pencils and acrylic paint glazes.   10 9 8 7 6 5 4 3 2 1

Library of Congress Cataloging-in-Publication Data
Wild, Margaret, date. My dearest dinosaur / by Margaret Wild ; illustrated by
Donna Rawlins.   p.   cm.
Summary: A mother dinosaur speaks to her absent mate, describing how she and her newly hatched babies are staying alive while he hunts for a safer place for them all to live.
ISBN 0-531-05453-5.   ISBN 0-531-08603-8 (lib. bdg.)
[1. Dinosaurs—Fiction.] I. Rawlins, Donna, ill. II. Title.
PZ7.W64574My 1992 [E]—dc20 91-46166

For Maurice Saxby, with love
—M.W. and D.R.

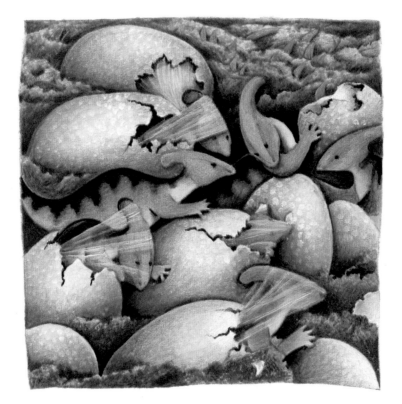

My dearest Dinosaur,
Such news! The eggs have hatched,
and we have seven little ones. I wish
you could see the wriggly, tiggly
rascals.

But where are you? *We* are here.
Here!

The little ones cling to my legs and neck. I tell them to be sure to stay close to me and not wander away from the nest. But the Cheeky One is naughty and bold. I am afraid for her. I hear noises in the night.

The little ones are growing bigger and stronger—and they are such good eaters. They ask about you, and I tell them how you went to search for a safer place for us to live, and didn't come back. They ask if you are dead, and I tell them what I believe. No. Never!

My dearest Dinosaur,
A Tyrannosaurus attacked at dawn.
I screamed at the little ones to
scramble into the river and swim.
Swim! The Cheeky One stayed by my
side until the last moment, squeaking
fiercely. It's a wonder she didn't get
trampled on. I pretended to be angry
with her, but really I am filled with
pride.

I could feel the Tyrannosaurus still watching us, waiting to snatch up my little ones. So now we are fleeing the marshlands, plunging through the forest, past the hungry snakes whose tongues flick in and out. My heart thumps, and I urge the little ones to run faster, *faster*.

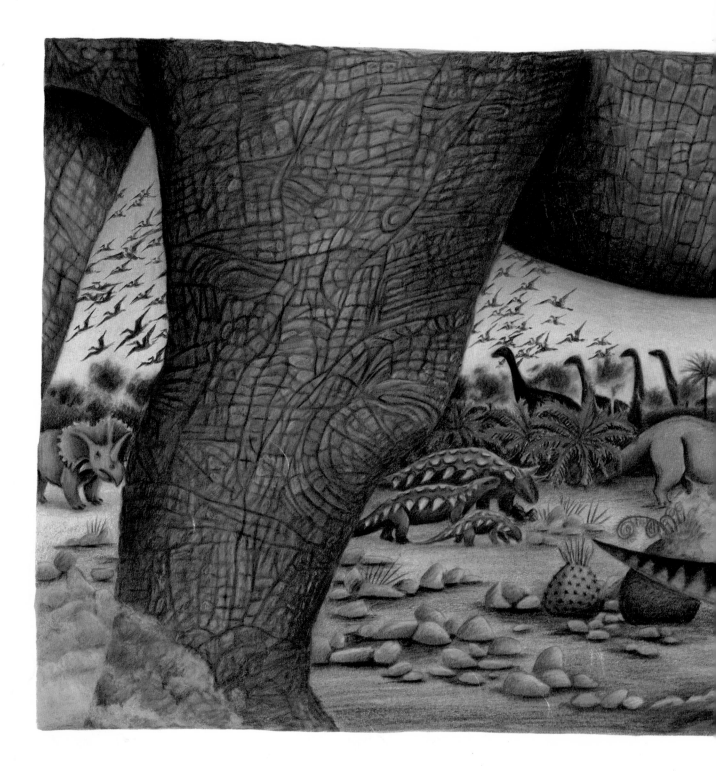

We are out of the forest—and safe. There are so many different fellow creatures here. Some with spines and frills and horns. Some with long, long necks and long, long tails.

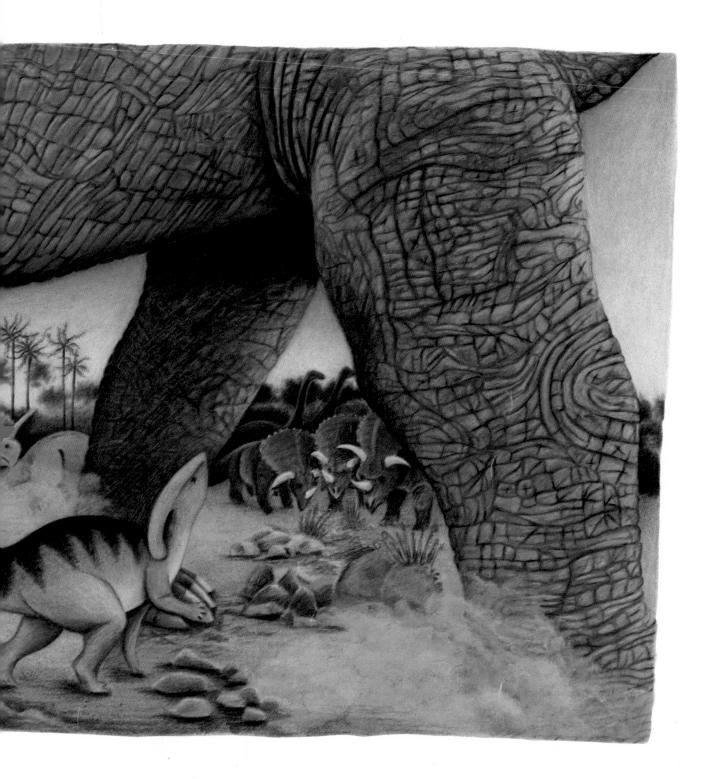

The Cheeky One is having a great time
scampering under the belly of the
Alamosaurus. I warn her she'll get stomped
on, but she won't listen.

My dearest Dinosaur,
The Cheeky One made rude noises
at a Dryptosaurus today—and was
nearly gobbled up. She's feeling very
sore and sorry for herself and has
promised to be good from now on.
We'll see.

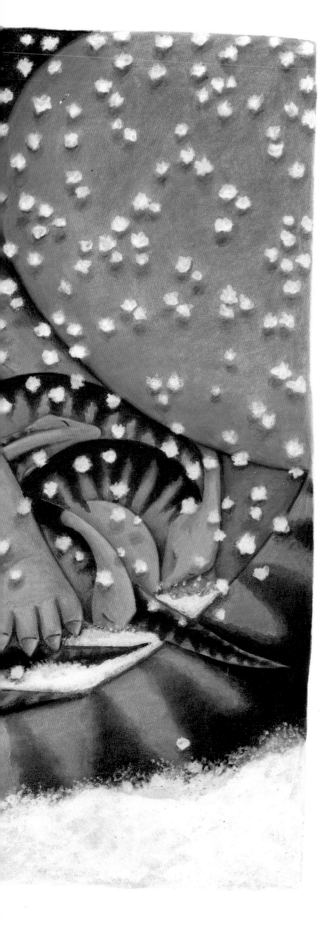

I had such a strange dream last night. I dreamed that something ate the moon and the stars and the sun, and everything was dark. I dreamed that wet, white flakes fell from the sky, covering the land. And there was no shelter. No food. I woke up shivering, and felt the warmth of my little ones against me, and I was glad it was only a dream. But what does it mean? And where are you? Where are you?

The Cheeky One has taken to playing with a baby Albertosaurus. I told her that these creatures are our enemies—that they like *eating* us. But she says this one will be her friend for ever and ever. If only it could be so.

My dearest Dinosaur,
The Cheeky One has left home! I dragged
myself all the way up the cliff, but I couldn't
see her anywhere. For hours I lay there at the
top of the world, watching the Pteranodons

circle and swoop. I told myself, over and over
again, that I always knew the Cheeky One
would be the first to leave—but why did it
have to be so soon?

The baby Albertosaurus keeps following me around, asking for the Cheeky One. It's curled up against me now, fast asleep, and I can't help liking it, the funny little thing. Perhaps it will somehow remain a friend. Perhaps the Cheeky One was right, after all.

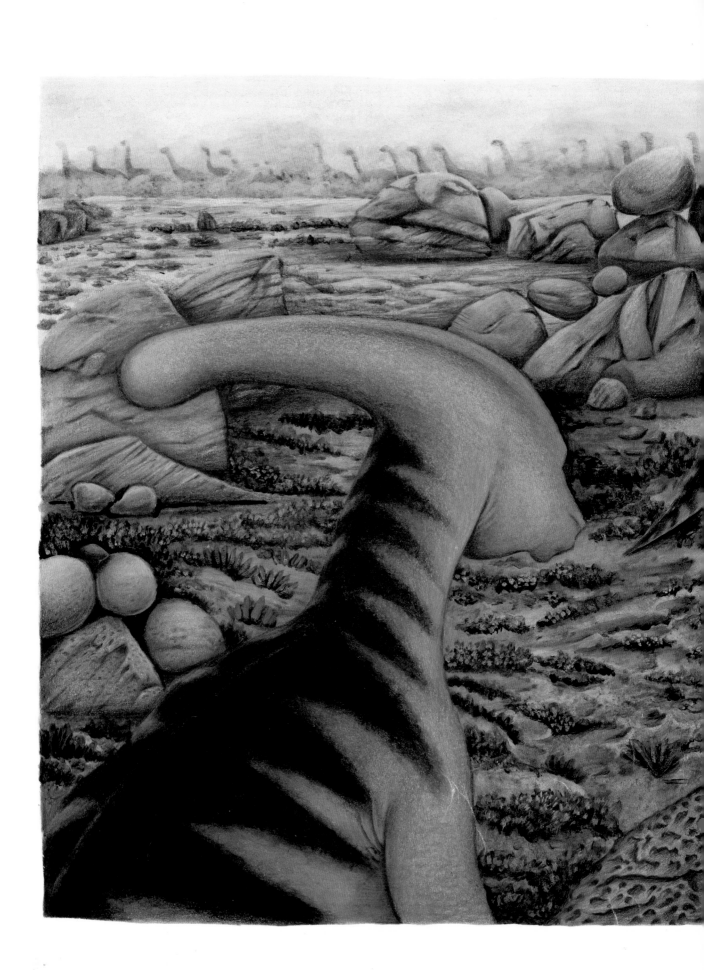

The little ones no longer need me. They are big and tough and impatient to leave my side. I watch them go and feel sorrow and a wild sort of happiness, because now I can come looking for you.

I shall search the marshlands
and the swamps.

I shall search the forests and the fields.
I shall never give up.

And one day—I know it—
we shall laze together in the sun, and
at night I shall keep you warm,
my dearest Dinosaur.